Births and Deaths in Ireland

Registrar General of Marriages, Births and Deaths in Ireland :

twenty-second annual report, 1885

Births and Deaths in Ireland

Registrar General of Marriages, Births and Deaths in Ireland : twenty-second annual report, 1885

ISBN/EAN: 9783742812339

Manufactured in Europe, USA, Canada, Australia, Japa

Cover: Foto ©Andreas Hilbeck / pixelio.de

Manufactured and distributed by brebook publishing software
(www.brebook.com)

Births and Deaths in Ireland

Registrar General of Marriages, Births and Deaths in Ireland :

twenty-second annual report, 1885

CONTENTS.

Page

REPORT

HIS EXCELLENCY JOHN CAMPBELL, EARL OF ABERDEEN,

&c., &c., &c.,

LORD LIEUTENANT-GENERAL AND GENERAL GOVERNOR OF IRELAND,

MAY IT PLEASE YOUR EXCELLENCY,—

I have the honour to submit, for your Excellency's information, the Twenty-second Annual Report on Marriages, Births, and Deaths in Ireland. The tables comprise all the usual details connected with the subject for the year 1895.

Some changes have been introduced into the arrangement of the present report as compared with its predecessors. Formerly Ireland was divided into eight "Divisions" for registration purposes, but as these divisions were found to have no practical significance with the public, and as their adoption caused considerable confusion in the compilation of the statistics it was given up in the year 1881, as pointed out in the eighteenth annual report of this department.

A further advance has been made in the present report towards the arrangement of the statistics so that they may accord with the recognised geographical divisions of the country. On this occasion for the first time the statistics of the Marriages, Births, and Deaths in Ireland have been arranged according to the recognised provincial and county areas.

This new arrangement has been adopted without discontinuing the system of classification by Unions or Superintendent Registrars' districts, so that the collective tables are strictly comparable for all local purposes with those hitherto published. It is scarcely necessary to point out that any arrangement, however correct from a geographical point of view, which would have deprived the local authorities of exact readily available information regarding the vital statistics of their respective districts would have tended to destroy the practical utility of the statistics. By the arrangement now adopted the twofold object has been attained of providing the public with a simple and comprehensive view of the principal vital statistics of all important and familiar geographical areas, and of furnishing local authorities whether urban or rural, with an accurate and detailed measure of the health of the people living within their jurisdiction, so far as such can be measured by the birth-rate and death-rate of the people.

It gives me much pleasure to report to your Excellency that the work of the

The Second Department of the General Register Office shows a steady increase in the amount of business transacted, thus proving that the records deposited therein are steadily becoming more appreciated and more availed of by the public.

At page 17, will be found a table which shows the amount of work done by the Second Department since the commencement of the Acts for the Registration of Births and Deaths and of Roman Catholic Marriages in 1864. It will be observed that the number of searches and of certified copies issued has increased with great rapidity during the past few years. This is mainly due to the demand for certificates of births, consequent on the requirements of the Board of Intermediate Education and the Senate of the Royal University. Another important addition to the number of birth certificates required has originated during the past year, owing to the fact that the twelve years have elapsed since the establishment of birth registration in Ireland, and therefore these certificates can now be used in many cases as proofs of their holders having attained full age. The demand for certificates of birth for this purpose may be expected to increase steadily, as the progress in the quantity of this department accumulates, a reference to the returns extending the earliest period of obtaining accurate information.

GENERAL SUMMARY.

The Marriages registered in Ireland during the year 1885 number 26,177; the Births 115,543; and the Deaths 90,712. Birth absolutely and in proportion to the estimated population, the marriages and births are under the annual average for the preceding few years; the death-rate is slightly in excess of the average.

The recorded natural increase of population, or excess of births over deaths, was 24,830; this sum by emigration amounted to 62,024; thus would this suggest to have been a decrease of 38,176 in the population during the year, but against a presence of this decrease there is a set-off in the migration of which an official record has been obtained. The estimated population in the middle of the year was 4,986,348.

Table I.—Showing for each of the years 1886–85, the estimated Population; the number of Marriages, Births, and Deaths registered, and the ratios of Registered Marriages, with the rates per 1,000 of the estimated Population represented thereby, and the averages for the ten years 1875–84.

Years.	Estimated Population in each Middle of each year.	Numbers Registered			Number of Roman Catholic Marriages	Rate per 1,000 of Estimated Population		
		Marriages	Births	Deaths		Marriages	Births	Deaths, Emigrants
1875								
1876								
1877								
1878								
1879								
1880								
1881								
1882								
1883								
1884								
Average, 1875–84								
1885								

MARRIAGES.

The number of Marriages registered during the year was 26,177, being 1 in every ten, or 4.30 per 1,000, of the estimated population, being 25 under the rate for the previous year, and 75 under the average for the ten years 1874–84.

Of the 26,177 Marriages registered during the year 1885, 14,300 were between Roman Catholics; 8,940 were celebrated according to the rites and ceremonies of the late Established Church; 2,542 were to Presbyterian Marriages; 315 to "Registered Religions" belonging to various religious denominations; only 447 by civil contract in the Registrars' offices; 8 were according to the usage of the Society of Friends; and 3 according to the Jewish rites.

Of the 8,940 Marriages according to the Rites of the late Established Church, 77 were by special licence, 2,909 by licence, 315 after the publication of banns, 31 on Registrar's certificate, and in 100 instances there was no information afforded as to which of the foregoing methods was adopted.

TABLE III.—The Number of Roman Catholic and of Other Marriages registered in each Quarter during the four years, 1882-85 :—

Quarters ending the last of	Province of Marriages Registered.							
	Leinster		Munster		Ulster		Connaught	
	Roman Catholic	Others	Roman Catholic	Others	Roman Catholic	Others	Roman Catholic	Others
March .								
June .								
September .								
December .								
Total .								
General Total .								

A complete registry of the exact ages of the persons married would be valuable from many points of view; hence it is matter for regret that in the great majority of instances the ages are not recorded. The requirements of the law are technically complied with by the entry in the age column of "minor" or of "full age," as the case may be, and there seems to be a general and increasing inclination to take advantage of this circumstance, as in 1885 the ages of both parties were specified in only 5,857 instances, being about one-fourth of the total number of marriages. In the year 1865, when 30,602 marriages were registered, the ages of both parties were given in 12,910 instances.

Of 21,177 men married during the year, 548, or 2·59 per cent., were minors; and of the women married, 2,211, or 10·53 per cent., were under age. These proportions differ but slightly from the averages for the preceding ten years.

The highest proportion of husbands (3·21 per cent.) married under age in 1885, was in the province of Ulster, and in Connaught there was the highest percentage of wives (12·64), not of full age.

It may be added that the percentage of persons married in Ireland who were under age is very far below the corresponding rates in England and Scotland.

The signatures of the contracting parties in the marriage registers or certificates afford a rough test of the progress of elementary education. In the year 1885, 16,133, or 76·3 per cent., of the husbands, and 15,619, or 73·8 per cent., of the wives wrote their names, and the remainder signed by marks.*

These figures, though still leaving much to be desired, contrast hopefully with the corresponding results eleven years since, the percentage of persons married in 1873 who wrote their names being—men 69·7, and women 63·3.

As usual, the most favourable results appear in Leinster, and the least satisfactory in Connaught, the number of those married who wrote their names varying from 81 in every 100 men and 81 in every 100 women, in the former province, to 67 per cent. of the men and 67 per cent. of the women in the latter.

In 5,082 instances, both of the parties married signed the register by "mark," and in 4,378 cases the register was then signed by either the husband or the wife, so that in 7,460 instances, or 35·3 per cent. of the total number of marriages, one or both of the parties signed by mark; and in 13,717 instances, or 64·3 per cent., both parties wrote their names.

The number of marriages registered in each of the eleven years 1875-85; the proportion per cent. of persons married who wrote their names in the registers; of minors, of widowers, and of widows are given in the following Table for Ireland, and for each of the four provinces.

In proportion to the estimated population at all ages, the registered marriages were most numerous in the province of Leinster, in which, however, the rate was only 4·7 per 1,000 persons; Ulster comes next, with 4·5 per 1,000; Munster third, with 3·6 per 1,000; and Connaught last, the rate being 3·0 per 1,000.

The highest rate in any county was 6·0 per 1,000 which was the marriage rate for Dublin; and the lowest 3·6 per 1,000, for Galway and Mayo. Between these, the most favourable were 6·5 for Antrim, and 4·9 for Down; and the least so 3·0 in Sligo and 3·1 in Clare, Kerry, Donegal and Roscommon.

BIRTHS.

The number of births registered during the year 1885 was 115,931—59,842 boys and 56,468 girls, or 1·05·8 of the former to every 100 of the latter—the rate afforded in proportion to the estimated population being 1 in 44·8, or 22·3 per thousand, which is considerably under the low average rate (26·9 per 1,000) for the ten years, 1875–84, and less than the rate in any of these years.

Of the 115,931 children whose births were registered in Ireland during the year 1885, 112,733, or 97·2 per cent, were legitimate, and 3,218, or 2·8 per cent, were illegitimate. The average percentage of illegitimate births in the preceding 10 years was 2·5.

It is unnecessary to say that these results compare very favourably with the returns for most other countries.

Of the children born in wedlock during the year, 57,604 were males, and 54,929 females, being 105·2 of the former to every 100 of the latter, and of the illegitimate children 1,678 were males, and 1,540 females, or 109·0 boys to 100 girls.

Comparing the provinces, we find that the percentage of children born in Ulster, who were illegitimate, was 4·3; in Leinster, 3·0; in Munster, 2·7; and in Connaught, 0·8.

TABLE V.—*The Percentage of Legitimate and of Illegitimate Births registered in Ireland during the years 1881–85, by Provinces*

Provinces	Proportion per cent. of Legitimate Births					Proportion per cent. of Illegitimate Births				
	1881	1882	1883	1884	1885	1881	1882	1883	1884	1885
IRELAND										
LEINSTER										
MUNSTER										
ULSTER										
CONNAUGHT										

The respective total birth-rates for the provinces in 1885 were—Leinster, 23·2 per 1,000 of the population; Munster, 21·8; Ulster, 23·8; and Connaught, 21·2.

The four counties having the highest rates are Dublin, 28·8 per 1,000 inhabitants; Antrim, 29·1; Down, 25·9; and Kerry, 23·1. Those with the lowest rates are—Monaghan, 17·7; Fermanagh, 18·2; Tyrone, 18·6; and Meath, 19·6.

Of the total births, 52·8 per cent. were registered in the first six months of the year (181 days), and 47·2 per cent. in the second half of the year (184 days).

The number registered in the first quarter was 30,344; in the second, 30,836; in the third, 28,119; and in the fourth, 26,662.

TABLE VI.—*Showing, by Quarterly Periods, the number of Births registered in Ireland in each of the five years 1880–84, and the average number for that period; also the number registered during each quarter of the year 1885:—*

Quarterly Periods	Yearly Number of Births Registered.							Estimated Annual Rate per 1,000 of Estimated Population.	
	1880	1881	1882	1883	1884	Average Number Registered	1885	1880–84	1885
First Quarter,									
Second Quarter,									
Third Quarter,									
Fourth Quarter,									
Total,					111,471				
Annual Rate per 1,000 of the estimated population,								—	—

DEATHS.

The deaths registered during the year amount to 90,712, being equal to 18·4 or 18·5 per 1,000 of the estimated population. The deaths of males number 44,880, and those of females 45,832, the former being equal to 18·7 in every 1,000 males living, and the latter representing 18·0 per 1,000 females.

The death-rate (18·4) is slightly over the average rate (18·3) for the preceding ten years.

As heretofore, very many of the Registrars furnished at the close of each quarter valuable notes on the sanitary condition of their respective districts. These notes were incorporated in this Quarterly Returns issued from this department, and inasmuch as they did, from genuine zeal, offered to speak decisively on the subject, it is to be hoped that their interest the various authorities of the various Local Authorities intrusted with the administration of the Public Health Acts.

With respect to the death-rates for the four provinces, the rate for Connaught is only 13·0 ; that for Ulster is 17·5 ; for Munster, 17·7, and for Leinster, 20·2.

Of the thirty-two counties, the five having the lowest registered mortality are—Mayo, 12·3 per 1,000 ; Cavan, 12·9 ; and Galway, Leitrim and Sligo, each 13·1.

Those in which the rate was highest are—Dublin, 27·4 ; Antrim, 22·4 ; Waterford, 19·3 ; and Limerick, 19·3.

The deaths registered in the first half of the year generally outnumber those in the second. In 1885, 57·4 per cent. of the total deaths were registered in the six months, January to June inclusive, and only 42·6 per cent. in the remaining six months of the year.

The annual rates represented by the deaths registered in each quarter are as follow—First quarter, 21·3 per 1,000 of the population ; second, 20·4 ; third, 15·1 ; and fourth, 16·9.

From Table on pp. 150-159, it will be seen that, of the 90,712 deaths registered during the year, 2,063 took place in Infirmaries and General Hospitals ; 880 in Public Lunatic Asylums, 11,093 in Workhouses and Workhouse Hospitals ; and 76,676, were of persons who died "At their Own Homes, &c." As in the Report for the preceding year an additional Table (see pages 160-161) is given showing like information for those Registrars' Districts in which the principal Urban Sanitary Districts in Ireland are situated.

TABLE VII.—Showing, by Quarterly Periods, the number of Deaths registered in Ireland in each of the five years, 1880-84, and the Average number for that period, also the number registered during each quarter of the year 1885 :—

Quarterly periods	Years and Number of Deaths Registered							Computed Annual Rate per 1,000 of Estimated Population	
	1880	1881	1882	1883	1884	Average Number Registered	1885	1885	1885
First Quarter, -								21·6	21·3
Second Quarter,								13·9	20·4
Third Quarter,								14·9	15·1
Fourth Quarter,								16·7	16·9
Total, -								18·3	18·4
Annual Rate per 1,000 of the estimated population,	18·3	17·1	19·4	17·9	17·6	18·1	18·4	—	—

B 2

CAUSES OF DEATH.*

I.—SPECIFIC FEBRILE OR ZYMOTIC DISEASES.

The deaths from Specific Febrile or Zymotic diseases registered during the year 1885, amounted to 8,165, or 166 in every 100,000 of the estimated population, being 23.2, or 5 per 100,000 persons, under the deaths from these causes in the preceding year, and much below the average for the ten years, 1875–84.

Of the 8,165 deaths from zymotic diseases 5,075, or 62.2 per cent, were amongst children under 10 years of age.

The deaths from the eight principal zymotic diseases† registered during 1885 form 7.9 per cent of the deaths from all causes, and are equal to 143 in every 100,000 persons living; the average annual mortality from the same diseases in the preceding 10 years represents 102 per cent of the average number of deaths from all causes, and is equal to 187 deaths in every 100,000 of the estimated mean population.

TABLE VIII.—Shewing the Number of Deaths from the Principal Febrile or Zymotic Diseases registered in Ireland during the ten years 1875–84, and the Average Annual Number for that period, with the Number registered in Ireland, and in each of the four Provinces during the year 1885, and the Rates per 100,000 of the Population represented thereby.

Years, &c.	Deaths from Principal Zymotic Diseases									
	Small Pox	Measles	Scarlet Fever or Scarlatina	Diphtheria	Whooping Cough	Fever	Typhus	Diarrhœa	Dysentery and Dysentery	Cholera
IRELAND.										
Average, 1875–84.										
Rates per 100,000 (population, &c.)										
PROVINCES, 1885. No. of Deaths	Leinster									
	Munster									
	Ulster									
	Connaught									
PROVINCES, 1885. Rate per 100,000 of Population	Leinster									
	Munster									
	Ulster									
	Connaught									

Small-pox.—There were but 4 deaths from small-pox—2 in Leinster and 2 in Ulster—registered during last year. The average annual number of deaths from this disease for the ten years, 1875–84, was 278. In 1882 there were 129 deaths registered; in 1883 the number fell to 16, and during 1884 there was only 1 fatal case of the disease recorded.

Measles.—Deaths from measles, which had fallen from 1,518 in 1882 to 801 in 1883, and to 559 in 1884, rose to 1,323, or 26.9 per 100,000 of the population, last year, the disease having been very prevalent in a few localities. The 1,323 deaths consist of 358

* In the year 1881, some modifications were introduced into the classification of the causes of death, so as to bring it into accord with alterations in Nosology recommended by the advance of Medical Science. These modifications are given in detail in the Eighteenth Report of the Registrar-General for Ireland, Page 5, et seq., 1881.

† Small-pox, Measles, Scarlet Fever, Diphtheria, Whooping-cough, Fever, Diarrhœa (and Dysentery), and Cholera.

in Leinster; 140 in Munster; 749 in Ulster; and 60, only, in Connaught, where nearly one-half of the total number registered in the preceding year occurred. 306 of the 338 fatal cases of measles in the province of Leinster were registered in the Dublin Registration District; 520 of the 749 deaths in Ulster occurred in the Registrars' Districts comprising the town of Belfast; and 126 of the 140 deaths in Munster were in the union of Waterford. So that in these three localities more than three-fourths of the total number of deaths from measles in Ireland occurred. There were also 33 deaths in Ballymena union, 25 in Lisburn union, and 22 in Enniscorthy union. It will thus be seen that in the far greater part of the country the mortality from measles was very light.

Scarlet Fever.—The number of deaths from this disease is 2,219, being a decrease of 249 as compared with the preceding year, and 453 under the average for the ten years 1875–84.

The deaths from scarlet fever in 1885 were distributed through the four provinces as follows:—Leinster, 587 (including 148 in the two Dublin unions, and 31 in Rathdown union); Munster, 626 (of which number 230 occurred in Cork county—including 54 in Bantry union; 84 in Clonakilty union; 80 in Cork union; 22 in Dunmanway union) 51 in Fermoy union; and 30 in Skibbereen union; 83 in the county of Kerry (including 58 in Killarney union); and 68 in Limerick county (including 24 in Glin union, just 24); Ulster, 745 (119 of which occurred in Belfast union, 51 in Larne union, and 49 in Millford union); and Connaught, 26 only.

In Leinster, deaths from scarlet fever corresponded to 12·5 per 100,000 of the population; in Munster, the rate was 23·2 per 100,000; in Ulster, 12·8; and in Connaught 3·5 only.

Diphtheria.—This disease proved fatal in 255 instances only, being 37 below the average number for the ten years 1875–84, and 58 under the number for the year 1884. In proportion to population the highest mortality (7·1 per 100,000 persons) was in the province of Ulster.

Whooping-cough.—The deaths (7,436) from whooping-cough are 881 under the average for the ten years 1875–84, and 398 under the number registered in the year 1884; they shew an annual rate of 29·2 per 100,000 of the estimated population. In proportion to population the mortality was highest in Munster and lowest in Connaught, the rates for these provinces being 34·7 and 7·4 per 100,000 persons respectively.

Fever.—The number of deaths from the several forms of continued fever was 1,854 (613 males and 369 females) being the lowest number registered in any year since registration was established in 1864; the average annual number for the ten years 1875–84, was 3,614; the number in 1884 was 1,993. The deaths recorded during last year are equal to a rate of 7·3 per 100,000 of the estimated population; the corresponding rates for the provinces being—Leinster, 8·9 per 100,000; Munster, 10·1; Ulster, 18·4; and Connaught, 30·1.

Of the registered deaths from fever, 805 were ascribed to typhus, 719 to typhoid or enteric, and 330 to simple continued fever, or vaguely as to "fever." The age-periods, 45 and under 50 years, and 65 to 70, were those at which fever proved most fatal in proportion to the living at the same ages; the former yielding a rate of 41·74 per 100,000, and the latter 49·77. The lowest rate was 25·21 for the period "under 5 years old."

Table 15.—Showing for the year 1885 the Deaths from the several forms of Fever at each Age-Period, with the proportion to the number of the living at each Age represented thereby.

Erysipelas.—The deaths from erysipelas number 263, being 30 under the annual average for the preceding decade, but 18 over the number in the year 1884. The highest mortality in 1885, in proportion to the population, was in Leinster, and the lowest in Connaught.

Puerperal Fever.—The number of deaths from this disease registered in 1885 was 370, being 63 in excess of the average for the ten years, 1875–84, and 70 over the number in the year 1884.

Infantum.—There were but 36 deaths ascribed to this disease; the number in 1884 was 43, and the annual average for the ten years, 1875–84, was 78.

Diarrhœa and Dysentery.—The mortality from diarrhœa and dysentery was remarkably low, the number of deaths being 1,264 (equal to 25·7 per 100,000 of the population), or 302 under the number for the preceding year, and 585 below the average annual number for the ten years, 1875–84.

The rates for the provinces in 1885 were as follow:—Leinster, 25·3 per 100,000 persons; Munster, 25·5; Ulster, 28·6; and Connaught 12·7.

Simple Cholera.—Twenty-two deaths were ascribed to this disease—30 under the annual average for the ten years 1875–84.

Four males and 3 females died from *Hydrophobia.*

II.—Parasitic Diseases.

There were 115 deaths caused by diseases of this class.

III.—Dietetic Diseases.

The deaths in this class number 162; they comprise 154 from intemperance, 52 of which (47 males and 5 females) were caused by delirium tremens, and 102 (84 males and 18 females) come under the head of chronic alcoholism.

IV.—Constitutional Diseases.

From diseases termed "constitutional" there resulted 16,499 deaths (7,848 males and 8,984 females), indicating a rate of 1 in 5·4 of all the deaths, and equal to 331 in every 100,000 of the population.

Phthisis or Pulmonary Consumption proved fatal to 10,799 individuals (5,044 males and 5,755 females), being equal to 212·5 in every 100,000 persons; the average annual number for the previous ten years was 10,426.

Its birthplace, Leinster and Ulster, yield the highest rates, and Connaught the lowest. The rates for the four provinces are as follow:—Leinster, 248 per 100,000 of the population; Ulster, 231; Munster, 178; and Connaught, 139.

Of the total deaths from phthisis, 7,927, or 73 per cent., were of persons between 15 and 35 years of age.

Deaths from Phthisis in the year 1885

Total	Under 5	5	10	15	20	25	35	45	55	65	75	85 and upwards	Rate per 100,000 living at each period
No. of Deaths	10,799												212·5

Mesenteric Disease.—The deaths from mesenteric disease number 1,017—595 males and 522 females.

Gout.—Only 28 deaths from gout were registered (21 males and 7 females).

Cancer, Malignant Disease.—There were 1,925 deaths tabulated under this heading, of which 872 were those of males and 1,053 of females.

V.—Developmental Diseases.

The deaths in this class amount to 19,237, of which 18,829 (8,797 males and 10,112 females) were ascribed to "old age." Of the remaining 458 deaths, 354 are tabulated under the head of "premature birth," 23 were caused by cyanosis, 35 by spina bifida, &c.

VI.—Local Diseases.

The number of deaths from "local diseases" registered amounted to 37,275 (18,511 males and 17,764 females), or 1 in 2·4 of the deaths from all diseases.

Diseases of the Nervous System.—From this group of diseases there resulted 8,255 deaths (4,056 males and 4,199 females). They include 3,606 from convulsions (nearly all children), 1,426 from hemiplegia (brain paralysis), 1,062 from apoplexy, 1,081 from inflammation of the brain, 349 from epilepsy, 245 from insanity (general paralysis of the insane), 49 (3 males and 12 females) from chorea or St. Vitus's dance, 243 from softening of the brain, &c.

Diseases of the Circulatory System.—Diseases of the circulatory system caused 5,027 deaths. 2,562 males and 2,465 females.

Diseases of the Respiratory System.—The deaths from these diseases, amounted to 16,000 (8,404 males and 7,596 females), being equal to 334·9 in every 100,000 of the population. The average number for the preceding ten years was 15,489, the annual numbers varying from 14,046 in 1880 to 16,604 in 1879. The respective rates for the Provinces, in 1885, are Leinster, 345·9 per 100,000 persons; Munster, 330·0; Ulster, 347·5; and Connaught, 312·3.

As many as 10,279 of the deaths from these causes (4,936 males and 5,343 females) resulted from bronchitis; 5,944 (2,807 males and 1,137 females) were from pneumonia or inflammation of the lungs; 707 from croup; 309 from asthma and emphysema; 234 from pleurisy; 192 from laryngitis, &c.

DEATHS from DISEASES of the RESPIRATORY SYSTEM in the Years 1875–85.

Year	1875	1876	1877	1878	1879	1880	1881	1882	1883	1884	Average 1875–84	1885	Rate per 100,000 living 1885
No. of Deaths	14,322	15,466	15,456	14,846	16,604	17,136	14,976	17,298	14,047	14,346	15,489	16,000	334·9

Diseases of the Digestive System.—These diseases contributed 6,273 deaths (3,471 males and 2,802 females). They include 474 from enteritis or inflammation of the bowels; 311 from peritonitis or inflammation of the covering of the bowels; 328 from ileus or obstruction of the bowels; 1436 from stoppation of the intestines; 160 from hernia; 7 (4 males and 3 females) from fistula; 230, 810 males and 88 females from cirrhosis of liver, &c.

Diseases of the Urinary System.—In the various affections of this order of diseases 1,430 deaths (1,097 males and 613 females) were ascribed. Of these deaths, 913 (907 males and 206 females) were from Bright's disease, 149 from nephritis or inflammation of the kidneys; 16 from ischuria or suppression of urine; 15 from stone in the bladder; 15 from uraemia, &c.

The remaining deaths from Local Diseases comprise 44 from *Diseases of the Lymphatic System* and 6 of *Ductless Glands*; 825 from *Diseases of the Reproductive System (including 469 from diseases of the Organs of Generation,* and 356 from the Accidents of Childbirth); 588 from *Diseases of the Locomotive System* and 579 from *Diseases of the Integumentary System.*

VII.—VIOLENT DEATHS.

The number of violent deaths registered during the year was 1,888 (1,289 males and 599 females), or 38·2 in every 100,000 of the population, being slightly under the average rate for the ten years 1875–84. Accidents or negligence caused 1,646 of these deaths (including 637 from fractures and contusions, 320 from burns or scalds, and 336 from drowning); there were 109 cases of homicide (murder and manslaughter), and 129 of suicide; 2 men were executed—both in the Province of Connaught.

DEATHS from VIOLENCE in the Years 1875–85.

Year	1875	1876	1877	1878	1879	1880	1881	1882	1883	1884	Average 1875–84	1885	Rate per 100,000 living 1885
No. of Deaths	1,547	1,844	1,855	1,843	1,794	1,972	1,849	1,966	1,943	1,994	1,870	1,888	38·2

Inquests.—There were 2,011 inquests reported to the Registrars during the year 1885, being 1 inquest to every 43 deaths registered.

AGES.

Deaths of infants under 1 year old numbered 11,033, being equal to 9·3 per cent. of the number of births registered.

Amongst children under 5 years of age 19,360 deaths occurred—a mortality equal to 35·3 in every 1,000 of the living at that age. Of these, 10,187 were boys and 9,143 girls; the former number representing 36·6 in every 1,000 boys, and the latter 33·9 in every 1,000 girls under 5 years old.

The deaths of persons aged 65 years and upwards are equivalent to 10·0 per cent. of the living at that age.

Amongst the deaths registered are 650 of persons stated to have been aged 95 years and upwards—818 males and 841 females.

EMIGRATION.

According to the Returns obtained by the Royal Irish Constabulary and the Metropolitan Police, who acted as enumerators at the several Irish seaports, the number of emigrants who left Ireland during the year 1885 amounted to 62,034; of these 30,873 were males and 31,161 were females. Of the whole number, 10,152 were from the Province of Leinster; 20,436 from Munster; 13,496 from Ulster; and 11,946 from Connaught.

Of the total emigrants from Ireland in 1885, 15·0 per cent were under 15 years of age; 73·2 per cent were between 15 and 35 years old; and 11·8 per cent were 35 or upwards.

PRICES OF PROVISIONS, AND PAUPERISM.

The average prices, in Dublin, of potatoes and bread in 1885 were similar those for the preceding year; the average price of Messrs. Manders' milk 4·3s. loaf was 6d., being ¼d. under the average price for 1884. Oatmeal averaged 17s. 6d. per cwt., being the same average price as in 1884; the average price of potatoes ranged from 2s. 4d. to 3s. 3d. per cwt., against 2s. 8d. to 3s. 6d. in 1884; and those of beef from 62s. 6d. to 68s. per cwt., against 62s. 6d. to 72s. in 1884.

Table X.—Average Prices in Dublin of Bread, Oatmeal, Potatoes and Beef, during ten years 1876-85, and the Average Number of Paupers in Ireland receiving Indoor and Out-door Relief on Saturdays in each year; also the Average Number of Paupers and the Average Number of Paupers in Receipt of Relief during each quarter of the year 1885.

Surveying the period covered by the several Tables in this Report, i.e., 1885, and the ten years preceding, it is found that beef was lowest in the year 1885, when the average prices ranged from 52 6s. to 66s. per cwt.; bread was also lowest in 1885, in which year the average price of Messrs. Manders' 4·lb. loaf was 6d.; oatmeal in 1881, when the average price was 14s. 1d. per cwt.; and potatoes in 1885, when the average range of prices was from 2s. 4d. to 3s. 3d. per cwt. The highest average price of bread was 8d. in the year 1877; of oatmeal, 17s. 10d. in 1877; the highest range for potatoes, 4s. 9d. to 7s. 6d. per cwt. in 1878, and for beef, 66s. 6d. to 77s. per cwt. in 1883.

From Returns, for which I am indebted to the Local Government Board, it appears that the average number of workhouse inmates in Ireland on Saturdays during the year 1885 was 47,009, being 1,232 under the average for the preceding year; and that the average number of persons receiving out-door relief was 58,631, or 642 over the corresponding number for 1884.

SEARCH DEPARTMENT OF THE GENERAL REGISTER OFFICE.

TABLE II.—Number of SEARCHES made, and CERTIFICATES issued at the GENERAL REGISTER OFFICE, DUBLIN, during the 12 years 1864–85, with the AMOUNT of FEES RECEIVED.

YEAR.	Annual Number of Searches made in the Registers.	Annual Number of Certificates.	Annual Amount of Fees received and paid into the Exchequer.	YEAR.	Annual Number of Searches made in the Registers.	Annual Number of Certificates.	Annual Amount of Fees received which paid into the Exchequer.
1864				1875			
1865				1876			
1866				1877			
1867				1878			
1868				1879			
1869				1880			
1870				1881			
1871				1882			
1872				1883			
1873				1884			
1874				1885			

THE WEATHER.

The following particulars have been derived from Returns of Meteorological Observations taken during the years 1885–86, at 40, Blackhamptonquay, West, Dublin, by J. W. Moore, Esq., M.D., &c., Observer at Dublin for the Meteorological Office, London :—

[The remainder of this section is illegible in the source image.]

TABLE XII. showing the Temperature of the Air in Dublin in 1854, and the Average Temperature for the Twenty Years 1835 to 1854, inclusive.

(Table of monthly and yearly temperature values — largely illegible in scan.)

N.B.—The temperatures given above were deduced from the combined and different readings of the Thermometer by Kinahan's calculations, &c., with a [Sum − min × ½] = Mean temperature.

I have the honour to be

Your Excellency's faithful servant,

THOS. W. GRIMSHAW,
Registrar-General.

GENERAL REGISTER OFFICE,
CHARLEMONT HOUSE,
Dublin, 15th June 1864.

ABSTRACT OF METEOROLOGICAL OBSERVATIONS taken at 10, Fitzwilliam square, West, Dublin, during the Year 1864, by J. W. Moore, Esq., M.D., Dun Tan, F.R.C.P., &c. &c. &c.

Long. 6° 15′ W.; Lat. 53° 20′ N.; Height above Mean Sea Level, 85 feet.) Thermometer, 8 feet above ground; Rain Gauge, 2 feet above ground.

Table showing the Monthly and Yearly Rainfall at Dublin during the Twenty-one Years 1863 to 1883, inclusive, with the Means for the Twenty Years 1863 to 1883.

Table showing the Monthly and Yearly Number of Rainy Days at Dublin during the Twenty-one Years 1863 to 1883, inclusive, with the Means for the Twenty Years 1863 to 1883.

ANNUAL ABSTRACTS

OF

MARRIAGES, BIRTHS, AND DEATHS,

1885.

ABSTRACT OF MARRIAGES.—Marriages registered in Ireland, pursuant to the

Acts 7 & 8 Vic., c. 81, and 26 & 27 Vic., c. 90, in the year ending 31st December, 1885.

MARRIAGES in the Year 1885—in Counties.

MARRIAGES in the Year 1885—in Counties.

MARRIAGES in the Year 1885—in Counties.

MARRIAGES in the Year 1885—in Counties.

Acts 7 & 8 Vict., c. 81, and 26 & 27 Vic., c 90, in the year ending 31st December, 1865.

MARRIAGES in the Year 1865—in SUPERINTENDENT REGISTRARS' DISTRICTS



MARRIAGES in the Year 1885—in SUPERINTENDENT REGISTRARS' DISTRICTS.

MARRIAGES in the Year 1885—in SUPERINTENDENT REGISTRARS' DISTRICTS.

The table on this page is too degraded to transcribe reliably. The column headers relate to "MARRIAGES" registered among the rites of the various religious denominations, with districts listed under the Superintendent Registrars' Districts including "I.B. CORK Co.", "I.C. KERRY Co.", "I.D. LIMERICK Co.", and "II. TIPPERARY Co."

II.—PROVINCE OF MUNSTER.—*continued.*

III.—PROVINCE OF ULSTER.—

MARRIAGES in the Year 1835—in SUPERINTENDENT REGISTRARS' DISTRICTS.

MARRIAGES in the Year 1835—in SUPERINTENDENT REGISTRARS' DISTRICTS.

MARRIAGES in the Year 1885.—in SUPERINTENDENT REGISTRARS' DISTRICTS.

MARRIAGES in the Year 1883—in SUPERINTENDENT REGISTRARS' DISTRICTS.

AGES of 10,714 PERSONS WHO WERE MARRIED IN IRELAND IN THE YEAR 1864

The Total Number of MARRIAGES registered in Ireland in the Year 1865 was 21,177; the precise Ages of both Parties were specified in 5,357 Marriages.

AGES of 5,357 MEN and 5,357 WOMEN married in Ireland in the Year 1865.

AGES of 4,838 BACHELORS and 5,101 SPINSTERS married in 1865.

AGES of 381 WIDOWERS and 256 WIDOWS married in 1865.

AGES of 5,357 HUSBANDS and their WIVES in combination in 1865.

AGES of 4,676 BACHELORS and 4,676 SPINSTERS who intermarried in 1865.

Ages of 157 BACHELORS and 157 WIDOWS who intermarried in the year 1845.

Ages of 525 WIDOWERS and 425 SPINSTERS who intermarried in the year 1845.

MARRIAGES, BIRTHS, AND DEATHS in each PROVINCE and COUNTY in IRELAND, registered in the year 1885.

I.—PROVINCE OF LEINSTER.—MARRIAGES, BIRTHS, AND DEATHS, 1885—COUNTIES.

II.—PROVINCE OF MUNSTER.—MARRIAGES, BIRTHS, AND DEATHS, 1885—COUNTIES.

III.—PROVINCE OF ULSTER.—MARRIAGES, BIRTHS, AND DEATHS, 1885—COUNTIES.

IV.—PROVINCE OF CONNAUGHT.—MARRIAGES, BIRTHS, AND DEATHS, 1885—COUNTIES.

MARRIAGES, BIRTHS, and DEATHS registered in the Year 1865.

1. PROVINCE OF LEINSTER.—MARRIAGES, BIRTHS, and DEATHS, 1865.

SUPERINTENDENT REGISTRARS' DISTRICTS, ARRANGED BY COUNTIES.[*]

(Where the number of entries is given in the bracket, etc.)

[The remainder of the page is a large statistical table giving Marriages, Births, and Deaths for Superintendent Registrars' Districts arranged by counties; the figures are too faded and low-resolution to transcribe reliably.]

[*] For detail concerning the numbers etc.

I.—PROVINCE OF LEINSTER.—MARRIAGES, BIRTHS, AND DEATHS, 1865—
SUPERINTENDENT REGISTRARS' DISTRICTS—*continued.*

[Table largely illegible due to image degradation]

II.—PROVINCE OF MUNSTER.—MARRIAGES, BIRTHS, AND DEATHS, 1865—
SUPERINTENDENT REGISTRARS' DISTRICTS.

[Table largely illegible due to image degradation]

III.—PROVINCES OF MUNSTER.—MARRIAGES, BIRTHS, AND DEATHS, 1895.—
SUPERINTENDENT REGISTRARS' DISTRICTS—*continued.*

CI.—PROVINCE OF MUNSTER.—MARRIAGES, BIRTHS, AND DEATHS, 1864.—
SUPERINTENDENT REGISTRARS' DISTRICTS—*continued.*

CII.—PROVINCE OF ULSTER.—MARRIAGES, BIRTHS, AND DEATHS, 1864.
SUPERINTENDENT REGISTRARS' DISTRICTS.

III.—PROVINCE OF ULSTER.—MARRIAGES, BIRTHS, AND DEATHS, 1883.—SUPERINTENDENT REGISTRARS' DISTRICTS—continued.

IV.—DIVISION OF COUNTIES.—MARRIAGES, BIRTHS, AND DEATHS, 1856.—
SUPERINTENDENT REGISTRARS' DISTRICTS.

MARRIAGES, BIRTHS, AND DEATHS REGISTERED IN THE YEAR 1885.

MARRIAGES, BIRTHS, AND DEATHS, REGISTERED IN THE YEAR 1845.

SUPERINTENDENT REGISTRARS' DISTRICTS OR POOR LAW UNIONS, ARRANGED ALPHABETICALLY—*con.*

Number of Parishes of Unions in prior-half Abstract	Superintendent Registrars' Districts or Poor Law Unions	Area in Statute Acres	Popula-tion, 1841	TOTAL			Births						Deaths		
				Marriages	Births	Deaths							Males	Females	

BIRTHS AND DEATHS Registered in the Year 1885—REGISTRARS' DISTRICTS, arranged by COUNTIES and SUPERINTENDENT REGISTRARS' DISTRICTS—*continued.*

			TOTAL									

BIRTHS and DEATHS Registered in the Year 1835. REGISTRARS' DISTRICTS, arranged by COUNTIES and SUPERINTENDENT REGISTRARS' DISTRICTS—*continued*

BIRTHS AND DEATHS Registered in the Year 1883.—Registrar's Districts, arranged by Counties and Superintendent Registrars' Districts—*continued.*

Superintendent Registrars' Districts	Area in Statute Acres	Popu- lation in 1881	TOTAL		BIRTHS		DEATHS					



BIRTHS AND DEATHS Registered in the Year 1885—REGISTRARS' DISTRICTS, arranged by COUNTIES and SUPERINTENDENT REGISTRARS' DISTRICTS—*continued.*

REGISTRARS' DISTRICTS	Area in Statute Acres	Persons living in 1881	Total		Deaths					Deaths		Excess of Births over Deaths
			Births	Deaths	Deaths of Impotent Stills		Marriage Season			Males	Females	
					M	F						

(Table data largely illegible due to page degradation.)

BIRTHS AND DEATHS Registered in the Year 1885—REGISTRARS' DISTRICTS, arranged by COUNTIES and SUPERINTENDENT REGISTRARS' DISTRICTS—continued.

REGISTRARS' DISTRICTS	Area in Statute Acres	Population 1881	Total		Sexes				Deaths		Number of Midwives Deaths
			Births	Deaths	Including Illegitimate Births		Illegitimate Births				
					M	F	M	F	M	F	
II. PROVINCE OF MUNSTER.											
7c Kanturk.											
1 Donnington, &c.,	31,663	1,100	611	100	79	78	1	1	500	40	13
2 Milltown Malbay,	4,703	9,463	471	100	114	146	·	1	72	45	71
3 Bradford,	20,307	6,370	317	71	46	20	·	3	63	86	6
71 Killarney.											
1 Ballyvourney, N.,	20,300	4,064	457	111	77	100	5	1	47	40	40
2 Lahmadaes,	70,013	4,564	115	6	54	61	2	1	53	43	13
VI Kilmore.											
1 Corrymboll,	33,300	6,747	163	74	41	42	·	·	35	96	30
2 Cappaghwhit,	30,200	9,863	243	143	30	47	·	·	9	40	32
3 Callan,	36,616	5,000	160	76	61	79	3	·	41	53	64
4 Lowvoild,	62,603	4,037	161	34	60	42	·	·	53	36	73
5 Mitrah N.,	30,100	5,167	370	170	103	160	7	7	63	42	53
71 Labinash, part of.											
1 Bridgetown,	61,156	5,166	200	6	43	66	·	7	63	30	32
2 Kirdowney,	71,566	4,673	41	63	54	47	·	·	32	70	70
74 Resheers, part of.											
1 Annascrough,	30,300	3,700	47	70	76	93	·	·	30	13	31
2 Foxlin,	34,670	4,061	100	43	65	306	·	7	75	11	64
3 Mountfinturough, part of, N.,	13,354	2,613	51	56	30	33	·	1	36	70	1
75 Trani.											
1 Aghalean,	31,446	3,316	36	46	63	36	·	·	23	36	36
2 Quin,	34,364	4,646	67	56	27	31	·	·	70	76	6
3 Tulla, N.,	37,065	4,671	76	70	47	63	3	3	64	96	6
South City.											
7a Bandon.											
1 Bandon, N.,	70,104	9,007	370	213	306	70	4	3	146	96	13
2 Innishanon,	13,360	3,011	64	53	36	76	7	·	30	36	3
3 Tullimckane,	16,604	3,734	47	46	47	33	·	·	79	17	33
4 Waragh,	13,367	4,600	70	46	64	36	·	·	56	36	6
5 Templemartin,	33,356	3,167	160	47	36	63	3	1	33	56	73
77 Bantry.											
1 Bantry, N.,	34,730	5,606	377	161	46	70	3	7	76	79	36
2 Eborian and Kilcrohane,	36,776	4,347	303	63	63	76	·	1	70	33	63
3 Innangasert,	37,630	3,611	66	36	66	37	·	·	74	16	63
4 Kealkil,	(small)	3,361	63	46	66	34	·	·	36	13	17

BIRTHS AND DEATHS Registered in the Year 1885—REGISTRARS' DISTRICTS, arranged by COUNTIES and SUPERINTENDENT REGISTRARS' DISTRICTS—*continued*.

BIRTHS and DEATHS Registered in the Year 1885—REGISTRARS' DISTRICTS, arranged by COUNTIES and SUPERINTENDENT REGISTRARS' DISTRICTS—*continued*

REGISTRARS' DISTRICTS	Area of Statute Acres	Pop.	Total		Deaths					Deaths		Excess of Births over Deaths
			Births	Deaths						M.	F.	
II.—PROVINCE OF MUNSTER—*cont.*												
(i) KERRY—*cont.*												

BIRTHS AND DEATHS Registered in the Year 1885—REGISTRARS' DISTRICTS, arranged by
COUNTIES and SUPERINTENDENT REGISTRARS' DISTRICTS—*continued.*

REGISTRARS' DISTRICTS	Area in 1881	Pop. before in 1881	TOTAL.							DEATHS.		
			Males	Females						Males	Females	
XI - PROVINCE OF MUNSTER, *continued.*												
105 *Kilmallock*, part of												
1 Cullolly,												
2 Kilmallock, part of												
106 Fermoy												
1 Ahern,												
2 Ardagh												
3 Doneraile												
4 Fermoy												
5 Kilworth, &c.												
107 Kanturk												
1 Ashgrove,												
2 Kilbrin, &c.												
3 Kanturk, No. 1, &c.												
4 — No. 2, &c.												
108 Youghal, part of												
1 Clonpriest, part of												
2 Gorse, do.												
Tipperary Co.												
109 Borrisokane												
1 Borrisokane, &c.												
2 Cloughjordan,												
3 Terryglass												
110 Cashel, part of												
1 Ballingarry,												
2 Ballingarry,												
111 Carrick-on-Suir, part of												
1 Carrick-on-Suir, part of												
2 Garrangibbon												
112 Cashel												
1 Cashel, &c.												
2 Fethard,												
3 Killenaule												
4 Kilcommon												
5 Fethard,												
113 Clogheen												
1 Ardfinnan,												
2 Cahir,												
3 Clogheen, &c.												
114 Clonmel, part of												
1 Clonmel, &c.												
2 Kilsheelan, part of												
3 Kilcash,												
4 Marfield,												
115 Nenagh												
1 Nenagh, &c.												
2 Newport,												
3 Portroe,												
4 Silvermines												
5 Toomyvara												
116 Roscommon, part of												
1 Roscommon,												

BIRTHS AND DEATHS Registered in the Year 1885—REGISTRARS' DISTRICTS, arranged by COUNTIES and SUPERINTENDENT REGISTRARS' DISTRICTS—continued.

4	Back Hill,	14,688	4,579	341	114	70	F
5	Tyrone,	29,788	3,889	319	67	88	6
	136. Dartmouth, part of.						
1	Featherstone,	25,872	8,283	199	116	88	F
	139. Castlereagh, part of.						
1	Cumnock, part of,	13,743	5,464	130	50	44	8
2	Knocknahattan, do.,	16,777	5,540	141	63	88	88
	139. Dundrum, part of.						
1	Summertown, part of,	5,288	1,888	68	31	39	11
	141. Ennan, part of.						
1	Loughs, No. 1, part of, W.,	5,600	15,098	448	509	888	31
2	— No. 2,	7,777	4,686	139	49	68	6
3	Pomeroy,	11,738	11,887	438	253	184	571
4	Tuckingham,	14,343	9,718	188	238	88	88
	142. Fivem, part of.						
1	Berdoll,	11,479	5,457	88	49	88	6
2	Hart,	55,833	5,347	308	90	88	8
3	Mannorhive,	17,788	5,188	88	98	88	88
4	Ballaghy,	14,111	9,488	718	188	888	88
5	Kilrey, No. 1, part of, W.,	5,418	5,863	919	271	189	888
6	Portaquad,	7,485	5,341	87	68	14	8
	Gaevan Co.						
	143. Barley witnesses						
1	Gulabmough, W.,	25,444	3,784	886	189	88	881
2	Creagham,	5,853	1,888	88	37	16	88
3	Kirennan,	13,887	5,888	68	84	88	88
4	Stranock,	11,278	5,069	78	88	44	88
5	Turann,	4,887	1,818	88	14	78	84
	144. Balteeven, part of.						
1	Ballymouth, W.,	28,884	5,188	111	98	48	88
2	Kemmaques, part of,	3,314	848	9	4	8	8
3	Gurtnahoe,	28,381	5,416	61	64	88	88
	145. Gobar.						
1	dough,	17,848	5,888	116	40	44	42
2	Gulghais,	79,354	5,448	74	44	41	88

BIRTHS AND DEATHS Registered in the Year 1885—REGISTRARS' DISTRICTS, arranged by COUNTIES and SUPERINTENDENT REGISTRARS' DISTRICTS—*continued.*

REGISTRARS' DISTRICTS.	Area in Statute Acres	Population in 1881	TOTAL		Births					Deaths			
			Births	Deaths	Males	Females	Males	Females	Males	Females			
XIII. SUPERINTENT OF WEXFORD—cont.													
87. Tyrone &c.													
188. Ardagh, part of													
1 Oakdon	7,880	1,827	44	72	44	34	1	.	30	13	75		
18. Castlebar													
1 Castlebar, W.	25,788	4,884	145	394	78	72	2	2	67	67	44		
2 Towngreen	77,734	5,390	62	37	35	27	1	.	18	16	38		
3 Kilbane	43,389	1,161	102	79	30	43	3	.	45	12	71		
190. Claremorris, part of													
1 Aughamoley, part of	30,176	5,412	67	193	34	33	.	.	39	16	32		
2 Ballinrobe	32,404	3,962	83	74	62	64	.	.	3	24	8		
3 Clogher, W.	31,813	6,390	114	115	62	43	5	1	73	42	-2		
4 Prunditown	52,297	4,420	79	36	44	34	2	.	36	27	38		
192. Crossmolina,													
1 Creagh	11,180	4,930	97	42	43	46	4	2	34	32	38		
2 Crossmolina, W.	33,979	15,409	594	321	123	410	3	13	112	73	9		
3 Ponteeny	34,734	7,432	110	38	64	44	1	5	62	43	10		
4 Bonnomore	34,862	3,471	138	34	36	65	6	2	41	43	38		
193. Dunreed,													
1 Rath-sogren	44,128	3,684	30	40	19	74	.	1	19	32	-4		
2 Boohan	44,340	4,641	107	98	38	43	1	8	34	44	4		
3 Clonroad	35,374	3,904	148	132	72	70	2	.	74	33	37		
4 Corn Imool	70,832	13,467	193	403	103	63	1	3	73	66	63		
5 Dungmore, W.	44,108	15,644	360	362	164	182	4	6	143	157	13		
194. Kabinatallon, part of													
1 Inatagh, part of	4,640	1,253	36	11	19	11	1	1	7	3	16		
195. Snert													
1 Tinnick, W.	44,504	7,354	132	394	73	70	2	1	34	30	61		
2 French Bridge	44,640	4,304	111	76	39	43	.	.	31	44	46		
197. Loughnashade, part of													
1 Ballinsmore No. 1, part of	4,172	338	8	3	4	3	.	.	1	1	6		
3 ,, No. 3, do.	14,850	4,388	74	40	40	34	.	1	12	1	72		
214. Outen													
1 Dromore	22,413	3,430	90	70	44	45	2	1	30	35	9		
2 Greenagh	70,083	4,104	62	38	33	34	.	1	30	33	14		
3 Fintona	17,397	7,760	143	114	73	73	1	4	83	42	11		
4 Omagh, No. 1, W.	38,160	15,413	304	364	143	146	16	13	173	130	34		
5 ,, No. 3	33,430	4,314	99	73	51	43	.	.	34	44	32		
6 Brookborough	48,642	3,762	111	76	36	37	3	.	34	46	31		
716. Strasbane, part of													
1 Dromore	33,083	6,130	173	44	74	34	.	1	63	31	58		
2 Newtownstewart	38,883	7,340	147	177	77	73	3	.	36	49	48		
3 Strabane, W.	19,873	10,814	309	138	176	183	34	43	164	73	32		



BIRTHS and DEATHS Registered in the Year 1885—REGISTRARS' DISTRICTS, arranged by COUNTIES and SUPERINTENDENT REGISTRARS' DISTRICTS—*continued.*

TABLES showing the NUMBER

of

BIRTHS

and

DEATHS

REGISTERED IN EACH OF THE FOUR QUARTERS OF THE YEAR,

also

DEATHS AT DIFFERENT AGES,

and

CAUSES OF DEATH;

IN 1835.

Note.—The Number of Marriages Registered in each Quarter of the Year 1835 will be found stated in the Abstract of Marriages commencing at Page 34.

..... registered in Ireland in the First Quarter ending

March 31st, June 30th, September 30th, and December 31st, 1853.

WALES					FEMALES					PROVINCES AND COUNTIES

BIRTHS registered in Ireland in the Four Quarters ending

SUPERINTENDENT REGISTRARS' DISTRICTS				MALES AND FEMALES			
			Total	Registered in the Quarter ending the last day of			
				March	June	Sept.	Dec.

March 31st, June 30th, September 30th, and December 31st, 1885—continued.

 marriages registered in Ireland in the Four Quarters ending

 I.—PROVINCE OF

March 31st, June 30th, September 30th, and December 31st, 1835.—continued.

March 31st, June 30th, September 30th, and December 31st, 1885—*continued.*

March 31st, June 30th, September 30th, and December 31st, 1865—continued

VESTRY—continued

MALES					FEMALES					REGISTRATION DISTRICTS

III.—PROVINCE OF

SUPERINTENDENT REGISTRARS' DISTRICTS	Area in Thousand Acres	Population in 1841	MALES and FEMALES				
			Total	Registered in the Quarter ending the last day of			
				March	June	Sept.	Dec.

Londonderry Co.							
174	Ballymoney, part of						
173	Coleraine, do.						
176	Newtown, —						
177	Londonderry, part of						
178	Limavady, &c.						
	Monaghan Co.						
179	Carrickmacross						
180	Castleblayney, part of						
181	Clones, do.						
182	Clogher, do.						
183	Cootehill, do.						
184	Dundalk, do.						
185	Monaghan						
	Tyrone Co.						
186	Armagh, part of						
187	Castlederg						
188	Clogher, part of						
189	Cookstown						
190	Dungannon						
191	Enniskillen, part of						
192	Gortin						
193	Irvinestown, part of						
194	Omagh						
195	Strabane, part of						

IV.—PROVINCE OF

Galway Co.							
196	Ballinasloe, part of						
197	Ballinrobe, do.						
198	Clifden						
199	Galway						
200	Gort						
	Loughrea						
	Mount Bellew						
	Oughterard						
	Portumna						
	Roscommon, part of						
	Scariff, do.						
	Tuam						
	Leitrim Co.						
	Ballyshannon, part of						
	Bawnboy, do.						
	Carrick-on-Shannon, do.						
	Manorhamilton						
	Mohill						

March 31st, June 30th, September 30th, and December 31st, 1835—continued.

ULSTER—continued.

MALES						FEMALES				SUPERINTENDANT REGISTRAR'S DISTRICTS
Registered in the Quarter ending the last day of				Total	Total	Registered in the Quarter ending the last day of				
March	June	Sept.	Dec.			March	June	Sept.	Dec.	



LONDONDERRY Co.

MONAGHAN Co.

TYRONE Co.

CONNAUGHT.

GALWAY Co.

LEITRIM Co.

births registered in Ireland in the Four Quarters ending

IV.—PROVINCE OF

		Area of Super-intendent Registrar's District	Population in 1891	BIRTHS AND STILL-BIRTHS				
	SUPERINTENDENT REGISTRARS' DISTRICTS			Total	Registered in the Quarters ending the last day of			
					March	June	Sept.	Dec.
o Co—					:		
21	Ballina, part of,	1,00,000	35,671	416	111	1,30	145	73
213	Ballinrobe, &c.,	1,54,145	23,900	305	145	138	514	118
214	Belmullet,	173,908	16,62	171	87	80	169	71
217	Castlebar,	104,700	4,107	700	715	113	140	155
218	Castlereagh, part of,	19,102	1,130	110	48	45	74	35
209	Claremorris,	114,700	34,308	605	220	156	452	271
220	Killala,	100,002	10,150	230	64	47	62	30
221	Newport,	170,054	19,535	184	104	85	53	505
222	Swinford,	151,404	54,114	4,377	452	268	611	887
223	Westport,	174,508	14,144	601	191	100	155	173
o Co—							
224	Athlone, part of,	44,100	17,114	450	117	145	47	48
225	Ballinasloe, &c.,	41,058	5,454	477	11	17	80	22
229	Boyle, &c.,	41,350	7,130	450	171	170	50	100
227	Carrick-on-Shannon, &c.,	47,445	4,107	145	45	80	52	50
229	Castlereagh, &c.,	105,330	30,300	545	170	458	155	145
230	Roscommon, &c.,	109,504	19,754	500	111	500	91	150
231	Strokestown,	50,055	17,552	504	507	54	150	41
o Co—							
214	Ballina, part of,	2,455	4,500	50	25	15	51	17
215	Boyle, &c.,	14,591	14,540	300	120	50	42	50
230	Carrick-on-Shannon,	50,500	17,503	450	30	75	50	71
216	Sligo,	144,500	44,503	504	200	54	303	445
215	Tobercurry,	175,171	34,171	504	100	50	157	150

March 31st, June 30th, September 30th, and December 31st, 1885—continued

CONFINEMENT—cont.

	MALES						FEMALES				SUPERINTENDENT REGISTRARS' DISTRICTS

BIRTHS Registered in Ireland in the Four Quarters ending March 31st, June 30th, September 30th, and December 31st, 1885, in each SUPERINTENDENT REGISTRAR'S DISTRICT or POOR LAW UNION.



March 31st, June 30th, September 30th, and December 31st, 1835

	MALES.						FEMALES.				DEPARTMENTS AND SUB PLANS DISTRICTS
Month.	June	Sept.	Dec.	Detd.	Total.	Month.	June	Sept.	Dec.		
											Carlow Co.
5	4	2	2	13	16	4	2	2	7		Ballinglass, part of
		3		4	2			5	1		Kilshenvaine, do
14	10	10	9	41	18	4	8	8	3		New Ross, do
											Hamilton Co.
											Ballieborough.

(Table illegible — heavily degraded)

March 31st, June 30th, September 30th, and December 31st, 1883.

registered in Ireland in the Year Quarters ending

I.—PROVINCE OF

March 31st, June 30th, September 30th, and December 31st, 1835.—*continued*

MALES					FEMALES					SUPERINTENDENT REGISTRARS' DISTRICTS
Mar.	June	Sept.	Dec.	Total	Total	Mar.	June	Sept.	Dec.	

...... registered in Ireland in the Four Quarters ending

III.—PROVINCE

SUPERINTENDENT REGISTRARS' DISTRICTS	Area in Quarter Acres	Families in ... houses	MALES AND FEMALES				
			Persons	Registered in the Quarter ending the last day of			
				—	June	Sept.	Dec.
Antrim Co.							
138	Antrim						
139	Ballycastle						
140	Ballymena						
141	Ballymoney, part of						
142	Belfast, do.						
143	Cushendun, do.						
144	Larne						
145	Lisburn, part of						
146	Lurgan, do.						
Armagh Co.							
147	Armagh, part of						
148	Banbridge, do.						
149	Castleblaney, do.						
150	Dundalk, do.						
151	Lurgan, do.						
152	Newry, do.						
Cavan Co.							
153	Ballyjamesduff						
154	Bailieborough, part of						
155	Cavan						
156	Cootehill, part of						
157	Enniskillen, do.						
158	Granard, do.						
159	Kells, do.						
160	Oldcastle, do.						
Donegal Co.							
161	Ballyshannon, part of						
162	Donegal						
163	Dunfanaghy						
164	Glenties						
165	Inishowen						
166	Letterkenny						
167	Londonderry, part of						
168	Milford						
169	Strabane, part of						
170	Stranorlar						
Down Co.							
171	Banbridge, part of						
172	Belfast, do.						
173	Downpatrick						
174	Kilkeel						
175	Lisburn, part of						
176	Lowtherstown, do.						
177	Newry, do.						
178	Newtownards						
Fermanagh Co.							
179	Ballyshannon, part of						
180	Clones, do.						
181	Enniskillen, do.						
182	Lowtherstown, do.						
183	Lisnaskea						

March 31st, June 30th, September 30th, and December 31st, 1835—*continued*
or *whatever*.

MALES						FEMALES				REGISTRY DISTRICTS
Ascertained in the Quarter ending the last day of				Total.	Total.	*Ascertained in the Quarter ending the last day of*				
March	June	Sept	Dec			March	June	Sept	Dec	

DEATHS registered in Ireland in the Four Quarters ending

III. PROVINCE OF

No.	SUPERINTENDENT REGISTRARS DISTRICTS	Area of District in acres	Population in 1871	Total	Registered in the Quarter ended the last day of			
					March	June	Sept.	Dec.
	Londonderry Co.							
171	Ballymoney, part of,							
172	Coleraine, do							
173	Londonderry,							
174	Londonderry, part of,							
175	Magherafelt,							
	Monaghan Co.							
176	Carrickmacross,							
177	Castleblayney, part of,							
178	Clones, do							
179	Cootehill, do							
180	Monaghan,							
	Tyrone Co.							
181	Ardee, part of,							
182	Castlederg,							
183	Clogher, part of,							
184	Cookstown,							
185	Dungannon,							
186	Enniskillen, part of,							
187	Gortin,							
188	Londonderry, part of,							
189	Omagh,							
190	Strabane, part of,							

IV.—SUB-PROVINCE

No.		Area	Population	Total	March	June	Sept.	Dec.
	Galway Co.							
191	Ballinasloe, part of,							
192	Ballinrobe, do							
193	Clifden,							
194	Galway,							
195	Glenamaddy,							
196	Gort,							
197	Loughrea,							
198	Mountbellew,							
199	Oughterard,							
200	Portumna,							
	Roscommon, part of,							
	Scariff, do							
	Tuam,							
	Leitrim Co.							
	Ballinamore, part of,							
	Bawnboy, do							
	Carrick-on-Shannon, do							
	Mohill, part of,							
	Manor....,							

March 31st, June 30th, September 30th, and December 31st, 1885—continued.

WESTERN—continued.

MALES						FEMALES				SUPERINTENDENT REGISTRARS' DISTRICTS
Registered in the Quarter ending the last day of				Total	Total	Registered in the Quarter ending the last day of				
March	June	Sept.	Dec.			March	June	Sept.	Dec.	

(table body illegible)

OF CONNAUGHT.

(table body illegible)

March 31st, June 30th, September 30th, and December 31st, 1855—continued.

CONTINUED—continued

MALES					FEMALES					SUPERINTENDENT REGISTRARS' DISTRICTS
										Mayo On.
										Roscommon On.
										Sligo On.

DEATHS Registered in Ireland in the Four Quarters ending March 31st, June 30th, September 30th, and December 31st, 1855, in each Superintendent Registrar's District or Poor Law Union—continued.

DEATHS Registered in Ireland in the Four Quarters ending March 31st, June 30th, September 30th, and December 31st, 1865, in each SUPERINTENDENT REGISTRAR'S DISTRICT or POOR LAW UNION—*continued.*

DEATHS Registered in Ireland in the Four Quarters ending March 31st, June 30th, September 30th, and December 31st, 1885, in each SUPERINTENDENT REGISTRAR'S DISTRICT of POOR LAW UNION—*continued.*

IRELAND.—Deaths at different Ages registered in the Year 1865—in the Provinces and Counties.—Males.

(Statistical table: Provinces and Counties of Ireland with columns for Males at different ages. The numeric data is illegible due to the degraded quality of the image.)

TABLE — Deaths at different Ages registered in the Year 1885 in the Provinces and Districts.—Females.

IRELAND.—DEATHS at different AGES registered in the year 1855—in the SUPERINTENDENT REGISTRARS' DISTRICTS in each COUNTY.—MALES.

I. PROVINCE OF LEINSTER.

IRELAND.—DEATHS at different Ages registered in the year 1865—in the SUPERINTENDENT
REGISTRARS' DISTRICTS in each COUNTY.—FEMALES.

I.—PROVINCE OF LEINSTER.

IRELAND.—DEATHS at different AGES registered in the year 1885—in the SUPERINTENDENT REGISTRARS' DISTRICTS in each COUNTY.—MALES—*continued.*

I.—PROVINCE OF LEINSTER—*continued.*

IRELAND.—Deaths at different Ages registered in the year 1865— in the Superintendent Registrars' Districts in each County.—Females—continued.

I.—Province of Leinster—continued.

IRELAND.—Deaths at different Ages registered in the year 1885—in the SUPERINTENDENT REGISTRARS' DISTRICTS in each COUNTY.—MALES—*continued.*

II.—PROVINCE OF MUNSTER—*continued.*

SUPERINTENDENT REGISTRARS' DISTRICTS																			
14. Cork Co.—																			

(remaining table data illegible)

IRELAND.—DEATHS at different AGES registered in the year 1885—in the SUPERINTENDENT REGISTRARS' DISTRICTS in each COUNTY.—FEMALES—*continued.*

II.—PROVINCE OF MUNSTER—*continued.*

IRELAND.—Deaths at different Ages registered in the year 1868.—In the Superintendent Registrars' Districts in each County.—Males—*continued.*

III.—PROVINCE OF ULSTER.

IRELAND.—DEATHS at different AGES registered in the year 1885.—in the SUPERINTENDENT REGISTRARS' DISTRICTS in each COUNTY.—FEMALES—*continued.*

III.—PROVINCE OF ULSTER.

IRELAND.—DEATHS at different Ages registered in the year 1883—in the SUPERINTENDENT REGISTRARS' DISTRICTS in each COUNTY—MALES—*continued*

III.—PROVINCE OF ULSTER—*continued*

IV.—PROVINCE OF CONNAUGHT.

IRELAND.—Deaths at different Ages registered in the year 1885—in the Superintendent Registrars' Districts in each County.—FEMALES—continued.

III.—PROVINCE OF ULSTER—continued.

IV.—PROVINCE OF CONNAUGHT.

Registration of Marriages, Births, and Deaths, Ireland.

IRELAND—DEATHS at different AGES registered in the year 1885—in the SUPERINTENDENT REGISTRARS' DISTRICTS in each COUNTY—MALES—continued.

IV.—PROVINCE OF CONNAUGHT—continued.

IRELAND—DEATHS at different AGES registered in the year 1885—In the SUPERINTENDENT REGISTRARS' DISTRICTS in each COUNTY—FEMALES—*continued*

IV. PROVINCE OF CONNAUGHT—*continued*

IRELAND.—DEATHS at different Ages registered in the year 1853—in the SUPERINTENDENT REGISTRARS' DISTRICTS—MALES.

IRELAND—DEATHS at different Ages registered in the year 1885—in the SUPERINTENDENT REGISTRARS' DISTRICTS—FEMALES.

IRELAND—DEATHS at different AGES registered in the year 1864—in the SUPERINTENDENT REGISTRARS' DISTRICTS—MALES—*continued*

Number of Marriages ...	Superintendent Registrars' Districts	Births Registered	Deaths Registered	MALES																	
										AGES AT DEATH											
				Total	1	2	3	4	Total	5—	10—	15—	20—	25—	35—	45—	55—	65—	75—	85—	95

IRELAND.—DEATHS at different Ages registered in the year 1865—in the SUPERINTENDENT REGISTRARS' DISTRICTS—MALES—*continued*.

IRELAND.—CAUSES of death at different Periods of Life in the Year 1864.—MALES

IRELAND.—CAUSES of DEATH at different Periods of Life in the Year 1885.—FEMALES

(Continued at page XII.)

IRELAND.—CAUSES of DEATH at different Periods of Life in the Year 1883—MALES

(continued at page 136.)

IRELAND.—CAUSES of DEATH at different Periods of Life in the Year 1885—FEMALES.

[Continued at page 136.]

IRELAND.—CAUSES of *Deaths in different Periods of Life in the Year 1885—FEMALES—cont.*

IRELAND—CAUSES of DEATH at different Periods of Life in the Year 1883—MALES—ctd.

(continued at page 140.)

IRELAND.—CAUSES of DEATH at different Periods of Life in the Year 1885—FEMALES—*con.*

			FEMALES.																
Class	CAUSES OF DEATH	All Ages	Under 1 year	1	2	3	4	Total Under 5	5–	10–	15–	20–	25–	35–	45–	55–	65–	75–	85–

IRELAND.—CAUSES of DEATH at different Periods of Life in the Year 1864—MALES—*con.*

IRELAND.—CAUSES of deaths at different Periods of Life in the Year 1883—FEMALES—*etc.*

IRELAND.—CAUSES of deaths at different Periods of Life, in the Year 1885.
MALES and FEMALES.

IRELAND—CAUSES of death at different Periods of Life in the Year 1885—MALES and FEMALES—continued.

IRELAND—CAUSES of DEATHS at different Periods of Life in the Year 1885—MALES and FEMALES—*con.*

Class	CAUSES OF DEATH	All Ages	Under 1 year	1	2	3	4	Total under 5 years	5–	10–	15–	20–	25–	35–	45–	55–	65–	75–	85–

(The remainder of this page is a statistical table; the figures are illegible in the source scan.)

IRELAND—CAUSES of DEATH at different Periods of Life in the Year 1865—MALES and FEMALES—*continued.*

DEATHS of Males and Females from different Causes registered in IRELAND, and in each of
the FOUR PROVINCES, in the Year 1885.

	CAUSES OF DEATH	IRELAND			LEINSTER			MUNSTER			ULSTER			CONNAUGHT		
		Males	Fem.	Total	Males	Fem.	Total	Males	Fem.	Total	Males	Fem.	Total	Males	Fem.	Total
	ALL CAUSES															

DEATHS from different causes registered in IRELAND, and in each of the FOUR PROVINCES, in the Year 1835—*continued.*

	CAUSES OF DEATH	IRELAND			LEINSTER			MUNSTER			ULSTER			CONNAUGHT		
		Males	Fem.	Total	Males	Fem.	Total	Males	Fem.	Total	Males	Fem.	Total	Males	Fem.	Total

(Table body illegible due to image degradation.)

DEATHS from different Causes registered in Ireland, and in each of the FOUR PROVINCES, in the Year 1865—*continued.*

Class	CAUSE OF DEATH	IRELAND			Leinster			Munster			Ulster			Connaught		
		Male	Fem	Total	Male	Fem	Total	Male	Fem	Total	Male	Fem	Total	Male	Fem	Total

DEATHS from different Causes registered in IRELAND, and in each of the Four Provinces, in the Year 1885—*continued.*

	CAUSES OF DEATH	IRELAND			Leinster			Munster			Ulster			Connaught		
		Males	Fem.	Total	Males	Fem.	Total	Males	Fem.	Total	Males	Fem.	Total	Males	Fem.	Total
VI.	GROUP H.															
	Carbuncle	71	17	88	7	5	11	5	6	11	9	1	10	1	1	2
	Phlebitis, Crinitis	23	16	39	6	7	13	1	5	11	2	9	9		1	2
	Lupus	1	13	13	1	2		1		2	1	4	2			
	Ulcer, Bedsore	41	9	35	16	14	30	16	11	36	13	14	14	1	1	2
	Eczema	73	11	32	3	1	9	7		13	2	1	10	1		
	Pemphigus	1		11					1		2		13			
	Other Diseases of Integumentary System	13	35	34	4	3	8	6	6	8	2	3	5	3		7
VII.	GROUP I.															
	Localised or Undiagnosed															
	Premature, Confinement	341	176	517	112	63	385	164	11	175	132	33	205	43	15	48
	Guarded Wounds	34	3	37	6	3	49	12		16	4	1	4	1		3
	Cut, Stab	3	3	15	4		9	1	3		4	1	3	1		
	Burn, Scald	171	299	300	13	36	169	39	33	97	38	36	177	30	30	33
	Poison	33	13	33	3	3	13	6	3	3	3	3	7	1		
	Drowning	377	33	330	33	13	33	33	33	333	33	33	33	43	3	33
	Suffocation	43	39	77	33	33	33	33	3	33	33	3	33	3	3	33
	Starvation	77	11	330	7	4	13	33	3	34	43	13	33	3	3	34
	OTHER J															
	Morbid, Homicpoison	39	39	330	33	33	33	73	7	33	38	17	...	3		6
	GROUP K															
	Suicide															
	Gunshot Wounds	34		34	3		3	3	3		3		33	3		3
	Cut, Stab	33	3	33	9	3	33	3	3	33	3	3	33	3		3
	Poison	3	3	3	3	3		1	1		1	3	3			3
	Drowning	33	3	37	3	3	3	3	1	3	3	3	4	3		3
	Hanging	33	33	33	9	3	33	1	3	33	33	3	33	3	3	3
	Otherwise	6	4	33	3	1	6	1	3	3	3	3	1		3	3
	GROUP L															
	Remains Unexhumed	3	3	3										3		3
VIII.	Dropsy	337	313	333	43	111	173	33	337	143	333	371	373	33	43	33
	Debility, Atrophy, Inanition	3,374	3,733	3,333	333	333	3,333	333	733	3,333	333	333	3,333	333	333	333
	Starvation	33	33	77	3	3	9	3	3	33	7	4	13		1	3
	Tumour	33	33	333	13	33	43	7	33	33	13	33	33	3	3	4
	Abscess	333	77	377	33	73	33	33	33	73	33	73	33	3	3	11
	Haemorrhage	33	33	33	33	33	33	33	3	33	33	9	33	3	3	33
	Sudden Cause Unknown	333	73	373	33	33	333	33	33	33	33	33	33	33	33	33
	Other Undiagnosed and not specified Causes	333	333	377	33	33	333	333	333	339	33	33	333	133	33	333

TOTAL NUMBER OF DEATHS.—NUMBER of PERSONS who died (1), in INFIRMARIES and GENERAL
OWN HOMES, &c., NUMBER of DEATHS from the PRINCIPAL CAUSES; and
REGISTRARS' DISTRICTS

and SPECIAL HOSPITALS, (2), in PUBLIC LUNATIC ASYLUMS; (3), in WORKHOUSES, and (4), at their NUMBER of INQUESTS in the PROVINCES, COUNTIES, and SUPERINTENDENT in IRELAND in 1883.

TOTAL NUMBER OF DEATHS.—NUMBER of PERSONS who died (1), in INTERMARRIED and GENERAL OWN HOMES, &c.; NUMBER of DEATHS from the PRINCIPAL CAUSES; and REGISTRARS' DISTRICTS

CAUSES OF

SUPERINTENDENT REGISTRARS' DISTRICTS OR

TOTAL NUMBER OF DEATHS—NUMBER OF PERSONS who died (1), in INFIRMARIES and GENERAL
OWN HOMES, &c.; NUMBER OF DEATHS from the PRINCIPAL CAUSES; and
REGISTRARS' DISTRICTS

SUPERINTENDENT REGISTRARS' DISTRICTS, OR

TOTAL NUMBER OF DEATHS.—NUMBER of PERSONS who died (1) in INFIRMARIES and GENERAL OWN HOMES, &c., NUMBER of DEATHS from the PRINCIPAL CAUSES: and REGISTRARS' DISTRICTS

SUPERINTENDENT REGISTRARS' DISTRICTS, OR

and SPECIAL HOSPITALS, (2), in PUBLIC LUNATIC ASYLUMS, (3), in WORKHOUSES, and (4), at their NUMBER of INQUESTS in the PROVINCES, COUNTIES, and SUPERINTENDENT in IRELAND in 1883—continued.

POOR LAW UNIONS ARRANGED ALPHABETICALLY.

TOTAL NUMBER OF DEATHS.—NUMBER of PERSONS who died (I), in INFIRMARIES and GENERAL
 OWN HOMES, &c., NUMBER of DEATHS from the PRINCIPAL CAUSES; and
 REGISTRARS' DISTRICTS

SUPERINTENDENT REGISTRARS' DISTRICTS OR

and SPECIAL HOSPITALS, (2), in PUBLIC LUNATIC ASYLUMS, (3), in WORKHOUSES, and (4), at their
NUMBER of INQUESTS in the PROVINCES, COUNTIES, and SUPERINTENDENT
in IRELAND in 1885—*continued*

POOR LAW UNIONS, ARRANGED ALPHABETICALLY

(1). in Infirmaries and General and Special Hospitals; (2). in Public Lunatic Asylums;
Principal Causes; and Number of Inquests in the Dublin Registration District,
Urban Sanitary Districts (those with a Population of 10,000 or upwards, in
the remaining portion of each Province.

Population of Ireland (including Army, Navy, and Merchant Seamen on shore or in port) estimated to the middle of each of the Years 1831 to 1865, inclusive:—

Middle of the Year	Recorded Population.			Middle of the Year	Estimated Population.			Middle of the Year	Estimated Population.		
	Persons	Males	Females		Persons	Males	Females		Persons	Males	Females

(The numerical data in the table is illegible in this scan.)

